GREAT TEAMS IN BASEBALL HISTORY

Hanna Altergott

Chicago, Illinois

For more information address the publisher:
Raintree, 100 N. LaSalle, Suite 1200, Chicago IL 60602

Printed and bound in China by WKT Company Limited

10 09 08 07 06
10 9 8 7 6 5 4 3 2 1

Library of Congress Cataloging-in-Publication Data:

Altergott, Hanna.
  Great teams in baseball history / Hanna Altergott.
    p. cm. -- (Great teams)
  Includes bibliographical references and index.
  ISBN 1-4109-1484-4 (hc) -- ISBN 1-4109-1491-7 (pb)
  1. Baseball teams--United States--History--20th century--Juvenile literature. 2. Major League
Baseball (Organization)--History--20th century--Juvenile literature. I. Title. II. Series.

GV875.A1A58 2006
796.357'64'0973--dc22

                            2005011484

Acknowledgements
The publishers would like to thank the following for permission to reproduce photographs:
Corbis (Bettman) pp. 4, 6, 10, 12, 16, 18, 21, 22, 23; Corbis (Hulton-Deutsch Collection) p.
15; Corbis (Reuters/Mike Segar) p. 42; Empics/AP pp. 11, 25, 26, 31, 36, 37, 38, 40, 43, 45;
Getty Images pp. 5, 7 (MLB Photos), 14, 17 (Time & Life Pictures), 28 (Allsport/Tony Inzerillo),
34 (Focus on Sport), 35 (Hulton Archives), 44; Library of Congress p. 8; National Baseball Hall
of Fame Library pp. 24, 29, 32.

Cover image of Derek Jeter reproduced with permission of Corbis (Duomo).

Contents

Welcome to the Game 4

1907 Chicago Cubs 6

1927 New York Yankees 10

1942 St. Louis Cardinals 14

1953 New York Yankees 16

1955 Brooklyn Dodgers 20

1961 New York Yankees 24

1974 Oakland Athletics 28

1976 Cincinnati Reds 32

1998 New York Yankees 36

2004 Boston Red Sox 40

The Final Score 44

Timeline 45

Glossary 46

Further Information 47

Index 48

Any words appearing in the text in bold, **like this**, are explained in the glossary.

Welcome to the Game

What would it be like to be on a baseball team that wins a championship or has a **dominant** record? Since the game of baseball began in the mid-1800s, there have been teams that stand out. Some of these teams have great players that can hit lots of home runs. Others use amazing teamwork. Some teams have managers that take a good team and make them great. A winning team isn't made from just one of these things, though. It is a combination of all of them.

This is a photo of the first World Series in 1903.

In 1903, the World Series was created and still happens every year in the fall. The purpose of the World Series is to find out which **major league** baseball team is the best each year. There are two leagues in major league baseball: the **American League (AL)** and the **National League (NL)**. The teams that win the most games go on to play in the league **playoffs**. The winners of the two playoffs compete against each other in the World Series for the championship. Today, both the AL and NL are divided into three divisions: East, Central, and West. Each team in both leagues plays 162 games in a regular season. Because of the different divisions and amount of teams, the playoffs today are a bit different from how they were in the past. However, the end result is always the same—a World Series champion!

Not all baseball teams have to win the World Series to be called great. The 1989 Chicago Cubs got all the way to the National **League Championship Series (LCS)**, but lost to the San Francisco Giants 4–1. The Cubs had some really strong players such as Ryne Sandberg, Andre Dawson, and Mark Grace. Today, we remember the team because of its great players instead of its loss to the Giants. Many outstanding players go on to be in the **Baseball Hall of Fame**. This honor usually happens many years after they stop playing baseball or after they have died. Managers can be in the Hall of Fame, too. With the amount of baseball players and managers in the Baseball Hall of Fame, you can imagine how many great teams there have been!

Since there have been over 100 World Series championship games, and lots of talented players and managers, the number of great teams in baseball history is enormous. This book chooses ten of those great teams and tells all about how they became the best. What kind of players did they have on the team? What was their manager like? Did they have a different playing strategy? How many records did they make or break? Who knows, maybe one day you will be on a great baseball team?

The Boston Red Sox celebrate their 2004 World Series Championship.

1907 Chicago Cubs

"Batter up!" This is what many baseball players hear just before they step up to the plate. The 1907 Chicago Cubs were no different—they just probably heard it more. Since they were one of the oldest teams in baseball history, the Chicago Cubs might have had the most practice. The Cubs **franchise** was created in 1870, six years before the National League itself was started. By 1900, the Chicago Cubs had won six National League **pennants**. The Cubs also played in four of the first seven World Series. Quite a feat!

ERA

The **earned run average (ERA)** is a measure of how many runs a pitcher allows over a nine-inning game. To figure out the ERA, use this formula: (earned runs x 9) / innings pitched.

Mordecai "Three-Finger" Brown (1876–1948)

Imagine being able to pitch a baseball with only three fingers! The Chicago Cubs' pitching **ace** Mordecai Brown did just that. When he was a child on an Indiana farm, Brown's right hand got caught in a farm machine. He lost most of his index finger and his little finger was paralyzed. Brown overcame his disability and used his unique hand in baseball. When he pitched with his three fingers, Brown put an unusual spin on his curveball and confused batters. He remains one of baseball history's amazing success stories.

Mordecai "Three-Finger" Brown throws a pitch in 1911.

In 1906, the Chicago Cubs had the makings of a great team. That year, they set a major league record with 116 wins and 36 losses in the regular season. A trio of future Hall of Fame infielders—Frank Chance, Johnny Evers, and Joe Tinker—helped the Cubs win the National League by twenty games. In the 1906 World Series, the Cubs faced their rivals, the Chicago White Sox. Nicknamed the "Hitless Wonders," the White Sox had won the American League with a strong pitching staff and a 93–58 record. Their hitting, however, ranked last in the AL with a .230 average. So, many people were shocked when the White Sox scored eight runs in each of the final two games of the 1906 World Series and ended the Chicago Cubs' great season!

Harry Steinfeldt, Joe Tinker, Johnny Evers, and Frank Chance helped make the 1907 Cubs a great team.

1907 Chicago Cubs

C	Johnny Kling	LF	Jimmy Sheckard	P	Carl Lundgren
1B	Frank Chance	CF	Jimmy Slagle	P	Jack Pfiester
2B	Johnny Evers	RF	Frank Schulte	P	Ed Reulbach
3B	Harry Steinfeldt	P	Orvall Overall	P	Chick Fraser
SS	Joe Tinker	P	Mordecai Brown	P	Jack Taylor

Manager: Frank Chance

C=Catcher, 1B=First Base, 2B=Second Base, 3B=Third Base, SS=Shortstop, LF=Left Field, CF=Center Field, RF=Right Field, P=Pitcher

1907 Chicago Cubs

The Chicago Cubs returned to the World Series in 1907, and this time their opponents were the Detroit Tigers. But their great effort in the regular season was starting to pay off. After Game 1 of the Series ended in a tie, the Cubs went on to win the next 4 games. The Tigers only scored three runs in those four games. The Tigers' outfielder Ty Cobb was usually a powerful hitter, but he had only a .200 **batting average (BA)** for the entire World Series. Game 5 ended in a **shutout** by Mordecai "Three-Finger" Brown. The Chicago Cubs ended the 1907 World Series with a championship and went on to win the 1908 World Series, too.

BA

The batting average (BA) is a measure of batting ability. To figure out the BA, use this formula: number of base hits / number of at bats.

This poster commemorates the Cubs' win in 1907.

Soon after the Chicago Cubs' win in 1908, the franchise began to go downhill. Although they still had great players, they struggled to make it to the World Series. In fact, the Chicago Cubs have only been to the World Series seven times since 1910. However, not many will forget the strength of the 1907 Chicago Cubs team.

A YARD OF THE NATIONAL GAME
Chicago Baseball Club. World's Champions and Record Breakers
Winners, National League Pennant 1906 and 1907, World's Pennant 1907

HISTORY BOX

Player and Manager

One of the key players on the 1907 Chicago Cubs team was Frank Chance. He was a talented first baseman. Chance was so talented, he was also the manager of the team; a position he took in 1905. As the first baseman, Frank Chance was on the receiving end of the Tinker-to-Evers-to-Chance **double play** combination. Shortstop Joe Tinker and second baseman Johnny Evers quickly fielded ground balls and threw them to Chance. The quickness and **precision** of this play earned it a place in baseball history. A New York newspaper even wrote a poem about them in 1910!

With talented pitchers and a solid record, they overcame a previous year's loss and came out the World Series champions. Maybe someday the Chicago Cubs will do it again!

1907 RECORD

Won	Lost	World Series
107	45	Beat Detroit Tigers 4-1-0*

Hall of Fame

Career Statistics	G	R	H	HR	RBI	SB	BA	Years
Frank Chance	1,286	798	1,271	20	596	405	.296	1898–1914
Johnny Evers	1,783	919	1,658	12	538	324	.270	1902–1929
Joe Tinker	1,805	773	1,695	31	782	336	.263	1902–1916

Pitching Statistics	G	W	L	ERA	SH	Years
Mordecai Brown	481	239	129	2.06	56	1903–1916

G=Games, R=Runs, H=Hits, HR=Home Runs, RBI=Runs Batted In, SB=Stolen Bases, BA=Batting Average, W=Wins, L=Losses, SH=Shutouts, ERA=Earns Run Allowed Per Nine Innings Pitched

*The middle number represents tied games.

1927 New York Yankees

Earle Combs, Tony Lazzeri, Babe Ruth, Lou Gehrig, and Bob Meusel made up the top of the 1927 New York Yankees lineup. They became known as "Murderers' Row" because they struck fear into opposing pitchers with their amazing hitting ability. The most famous of these hitters was George Herman "Babe" Ruth. Previously a pitcher with the Boston Red Sox, Ruth was sold to the Yankees in 1920 and left a lasting mark on the New York Yankees franchise and baseball history. Even today, some people think of Babe Ruth as the best baseball player in the history of the sport.

Babe Ruth had a great season for the Yankees in 1927. After coming to the Yankees, Ruth gave up pitching and played the right field position instead. His hitting became a force, and during the season he had sixty home runs. When talking about his new record, Babe Ruth said "Sixty! Count 'em, sixty! Let someone match that!"

Lou Gehrig and Babe Ruth select their bats.

George Herman "Babe" Ruth (1895–1948)

At the beginning of the 1920s, Babe Ruth helped shape the sport of baseball into something bigger. By hitting 54 home runs in 1920, and then another 59 the following year, Ruth created a whole new way of playing that involved lots of power and hits. Babe Ruth was also a big man, especially for his time. He was over 6 feet tall and had a powerful body when he was young. Ruth loved the sport of baseball and had great respect for his fans. He became a hero for both young and old people throughout the United States. By the mid-1920s, Babe Ruth was known around the world, even in places where baseball was not popular.

1927 New York Yankees

C	Pat Collins	LF	Bob Meusel	P	Herb Pennock
1B	Lou Gehrig	CF	Earle Combs	P	Urban Shocker
2B	Tony Lazzeri	RF	Babe Ruth	P	Dutch Ruether
B	Joe Dugan	P	Waite Hoyt	P	George Pipgras
SS	Mark Koenig	P	Wilcy Moore	P	Myles Thomas

Manager: Miller Huggins

It would take decades for a baseball player to "match that!" Babe Ruth had a total of 714 career home runs. In fact, Ruth hit more home runs by himself than the other seven teams in the American League! Lou Gehrig, a 24-year-old first baseman, was second in the AL with 47 home runs, and the Yankees' second baseman, Tony Lazzeri, was third in the league with 18 home runs.

With Ruth batting third and Gehrig batting fourth, the Yankees were unstoppable. Gehrig had 175 **runs batted in (RBIs)** and Babe Ruth had 164 RBIs. Babe Ruth and Lou Gehrig weren't the only super hitters, though. Lazzeri and Meusel each had over 100 RBIs, and Earle Combs had a .356 BA.

Babe Ruth hits another home run in 1927.

1927 New York Yankees

The 1927 New York Yankees also had a great pitching staff, with Waite Hoyt, Herb Pennock, and Wilcy Moore. Early in the season, manager Miller Huggins started using **rookie** pitcher Moore in tough games toward the later innings. Moore would provide "relief" for the starting pitchers in the games. At this time, starting pitchers played most of the game and the idea of a "closing" or "relief" pitcher did not exist. Huggins kept using Moore in this type of strategy and it eventually paid off. With excellent hitters and well-rested pitchers, the Yankees had 110 wins in the 1927 season.

This is a team photo of the 1927 New York Yankees.

1927 RECORD

Won	Lost	World Series
110	44	Beat Pittsburgh Pirates 4–0

Hall of Fame

Career Statistics	G	R	H	HR	RBI	SB	BA	Years
Lou Gehrig	2,164	1,888	2,721	493	1,990	102	.340	1923–1939
Tony Lazzeri	1,739	986	1,840	178	1,191	148	.292	1926–1939
Earle Combs	1,454	1,186	1,866	58	629	96	.325	1924–1935
Babe Ruth	2,503	2,174	2,873	714	2,211	123	.342	1914–1935

Pitching Statistics	G	W	L	ERA	SH	Years
Waite Hoyt	674	237	182	3.59	26	1918–1938
Herb Pennock	617	240	162	3.61	35	1912–1934

Manager: Miller Huggins   Won 1,413   Lost 1,134   1913–1929

The Yankees were confident going into the 1927 World Series against the Pittsburgh Pirates. Although the Pirates led the NL with a .305 BA, they couldn't match the power of "Murderers' Row." In Game 1 in Pittsburgh, the Yankees defeated the Pirates 5–4. Ruth had three hits for the Yankees. Game 2 went pretty much the same way as Pittsburgh only scored 2 runs, and the Yankees won 6–2. Back in New York, Games 3 and 4 sealed the Pirates' fate. The Yankees won Game 3, 8–1 and Game 4, 4–3 and grabbed the World Series championship. Not many people would be able to forget the power **sluggers** and the talent of the 1927 New York Yankees!

HISTORY BOX

A Clean Sweep

The New York Yankees made baseball history in 1927 for many different reasons. They were the first team in the AL to **sweep** a World Series. The Yankees beat the Pittsburgh Pirates 4–0 and claimed a record as well as a championship. The Yankees would go on to sweep the 1928 World Series 4–0 against the St. Louis Cardinals, too.

1942 St. Louis Cardinals

While the New York Yankees dominated the American League from 1920 to 1950, the teams in the National League built great teams to challenge them. In 1942, the St. Louis Cardinals was one of those teams. The Cardinals won the World Series in 1942 and two more Series in a five-year span. The team had a lot of great players including hitter Stan Musial, shortstop Marty Marion, and pitcher Mort Cooper.

The 1942 St. Louis Cardinals pose for a team photo.

The World Series opened in St. Louis with the New York Yankees scoring five runs in the first eight innings of Game 1, against Mort Cooper of all pitchers! The Yankees added 2 more runs in the ninth inning to win Game 1 of the Series by the score of 7–4. The Cardinals would need to play harder in order to beat the determined Yankees. With Cooper beaten, the Cardinals turned to rookie pitcher Johnny Beazely in Game 2. With solid pitching by Beazely, the Cardinals beat the Yankees in Game 2 with a score of 4–3.

1942 RECORD

Won	Lost	World Series
106	48	Beat New York Yankees 4–1

Hall of Fame

Career Statistics	G	R	H	HR	RBI	SB	BA	Years
Enos Slaughter	2,380	1,247	2,383	169	1,304	71	.300	1938–1959
Stan Musial	3,026	1,949	3,630	475	1,951	78	.331	1941–1963

1942 St. Louis Cardinals

C	Walker Cooper	CF	Terry Moore	P	Ernie White
1B	Johnny Hopp	RF	Enos Slaughter	P	Murry Dickson
2B	Jimmy Brown	P	Mort Cooper	P	Howie Krist
3B	Whitey Kurowski	P	Johnny Beazely	P	Howie Pollet
SS	Marty Marion	P	Harry Gumbert		
LF	Stan Musial	P	Max Lanier		

Manager: Billy Southworth

The Cardinals won the next two games in New York, including a shutout by Cardinals' pitcher Ernie White. In Game 5, Cardinals' pitcher Johnny Beazely was able to repeat what he did in Game 2 of the series. Having a record of 21 wins and 6 losses in the regular season, Beazely allowed only 2 runs on 7 hits in 9 innings. His solid pitching helped the Cardinals' win their fourth World Series title. The Cardinals would eventually go on to win two more Series titles in the 1940s.

Cardinals' pitchers Lanier, White, Cooper, Beasely, and Gumbert line up in the dugout.

15

1953 New York Yankees

In the first half of the 20th century, the New York Yankees were a huge force in the game of baseball. The Yankees' individual players as well as the team dominated baseball record books. Each season brought new and more talented players onto the team. During the 1920s, Babe Ruth was the dominant force on the Yankees. In the 1930s, it was Lou Gehrig and eventually Joe DiMaggio. When Joe DiMaggio retired in 1951, his replacement was center fielder Mickey Mantle. Of all the great Yankees players, Mickey Mantle might have been the best. Mantle was a great slugger and could run the bases at lightning speed. He hit 536 home runs in his baseball career.

Members of the 1953 Yankees team pose for a photo.

1953 New York Yankees

C	Yogi Berra	CF	Mickey Mantle	P	Allie Reynolds
1B	Joe Collins	RF	Hank Bauer	P	Jim McDonald
2B	Billy Martin	P	Whitey Ford	P	Bob Kuzava
3B	Gil McDougald	P	Johnny Sain	P	Tom Gorman
SS	Phil Rizzuto	P	Vic Raschi		
LF	Gene Woodling	P	Ed Lopat		

Manager: Casey Stengel

Changing Times

During the 1950s, many changes were happening in baseball. In 1951, the American League celebrated its 50th anniversary. That same year, major league baseball celebrated its 75th! Television began playing major league games more, and this caused less people to go see their local minor league teams. Major league baseball was becoming more popular.

A number of injuries eventually slowed Mantle's career down, but he kept his powerful hitting ability for nearly two decades. As a strong player on the 1953 Yankees lineup, Mantle helped bring the Yankees their fifth World Series title in a row. Fellow Hall of Fame catcher, Yogi Berra, joined Mantle. Berra was also a hitting force. In 1953, he led the Yankees with 27 home runs and 108 RBIs. Berra joined the Yankees team in 1946 and went on to play eighteen seasons with them. From 1949 to 1958, Yogi Berra hit twenty or more home runs in ten straight seasons.

The 1953 New York Yankees lineup was not just another "Murderers' Row," with hard hitters and little else. The Yankees also had a great pitching staff to support their sluggers. The main members of this pitching staff were Allie Reynolds, Vic Raschi, and Eddie Lopat. In 1950, another pitcher, named Whitey Ford, was added to the lineup. Ford missed the 1951 and 1952 seasons because he was serving in the military. In 1953, he was ready to make his mark on the Yankees team and baseball history. Ford won eighteen games in 1953. Today, with 236 wins, Ford still has the most career wins in New York Yankees history.

Whitey Ford pitches a fastball.

1953 New York Yankees

The manager behind the powerful 1953 Yankees team was Casey Stengel. Stengel led the Yankees to the World Series ten times. The Yankees won seven of those World Series. Stengel was an effective manager with a great sense of humor. He had a funny way with words, and he came up with phrases that left newspaper reporters scratching their heads in confusion. "Most ballgames are lost, not won," Stengel would sometimes say. If there is one winner in every baseball game, what did he mean?

With a team of great hitters, solid pitchers, and a good manager, the 1953 Yankees led the American League in runs, batting average, and earned run average. During the 1953 regular season, the Yankees had 99 wins and 52 losses. They finished first in the AL, with the Cleveland Browns a close second. The Yankees advanced to the World Series and set out to beat their National League opponent, the Brooklyn Dodgers.

The Yankees won the first two games in the Series at Yankee Stadium. The Dodgers responded to this defeat by winning the next two games. Pitcher Whitey Ford lost Game 4 in the Series, giving him a rare post-season loss. The Yankees would need to play harder in order to beat the Dodgers. In Game 5, Mantle hit a **grand slam** and gave the Yankees a lead that would not be caught. The team won the game 11–7 and went on to play Game 6 back in Yankee Stadium. Yankees' second baseman Billy Martin stepped up in the game with a single that led Hank Bauer in to home plate. The Yankees won Game 6, 4–3 and the World Series championship!

Yankees' Berra attempts to stop Jackie Robinson from crossing the plate.

Casey Stengel (1890–1975)

Born in Kansas City, Missouri, Casey Stengel had a major league career that involved both playing and managing and that lasted 54 years. It was his managing career that earned him a place in the Baseball Hall of Fame. With ten championships, he holds the record for most World Series titles by a manager. Stengel loved to tell jokes and make people laugh. He is still an inspiration to baseball players and managers today.

With five World Series championships in a row, the 1953 New York Yankees were an incredible team. The team and its talented players went on to be in the Baseball Hall of Fame. The strength of the Yankees in the first half of the 20th century was unmatched. With players such as Ruth, Mantle, Ford, DiMaggio, Berra, and many others, some people think the New York Yankees could be the greatest baseball franchise of all time.

1953 RECORD

Won	Lost	World Series
99	52	Beat Brooklyn Dodgers 4–2

Hall of Fame

Career Statistics	G	R	H	HR	RBI	SB	BA	Years
Yogi Berra	2,120	1,175	2,150	358	1,430	30	.285	1946–1965
Phil Rizzuto	1,661	877	1,588	38	562	149	.273	1941–1956
Mickey Mantle	2,401	1,677	2,415	536	1,509	153	.298	1951–1968
Johnny Mize	1,884	1,118	2,011	359	1,337	28	.312	1936–1953

Pitching Statistics	G	W	L	ERA	SH	Years
Whitey Ford	498	236	106	2.74	45	1950–1967

Manager: Casey Stengel   Won 1,926   Lost 1,867   1934–1965

1955 Brooklyn Dodgers

Many obstacles can get in the way of a great baseball team winning a World Series. Players get injured and teams sometimes just have bad luck or play a couple of bad games. For the Brooklyn Dodgers, these things seemed simple compared to their obstacle. The Dodgers had one team blocking them from winning a World Series. That team was the New York Yankees.

In 1941, 1947, 1949, 1952, and 1953, the Brooklyn Dodgers were the best team in the National League and made it to the World Series. At each of these Series, the Yankees were waiting to defeat the Dodgers—and defeat them they did. The Yankees won every single of these World Series match-ups against the Dodgers. In 1955, however, this all changed.

A good measurement of a team's quality is how strong they are in the four most difficult defensive positions "up the middle." Catcher, shortstop, second base, and center field are the positions that can make or break a team. The 1950s Dodgers team was excellent "up the middle." They might even have been better in these positions than any other team in history. From the years 1949 to 1956, future Hall of Famers dominated the "up the middle" positions on the Brooklyn Dodgers team.

1955 Brooklyn Dodgers

C	Roy Campanella	CF	Duke Snider	P	Karl Spooner
1B	Gil Hodges	RF	Carl Furillo	P	Clem Labine
2B	Jim Gilliam	P	Don Newcombe	P	Roger Craig
3B	Jackie Robinson	P	Carl Erskine	P	Ed Roebuck
SS	Pee Wee Reese	P	Johnny Podres		
LF	Sandy Amoros	P	Billy Loes		

Manager: Walter Alston

Duke Snider was out in center field for over a decade, beginning in 1949. Snider was an amazing outfielder with incredible speed. He was also the key power hitter in Brooklyn's lineup. Snider hit 40 or more home runs a year from 1953 to 1957. Shortstop Pee Wee Reese and second baseman Jackie Robinson made the infield strong. Their double play combo was unstoppable. Both men were aggressive, speedy base runners. Jackie Robinson batted a .256 during the 1955 season.

Behind the plate, catcher Roy Campanella was a master at both handling pitchers and hitting with tremendous power. Together, Reese, Robinson, Snider, and Campanella formed a strong Brooklyn offense and defense. When October of the 1955 season arrived, the team was ready. The Dodgers had finished first in the National League and they were more than prepared to meet their rivals in the World Series.

The 1955 Brooklyn Dodgers pose for a team photo.

21

The Dodgers went up against the Yankees in a fierce battle. The first two games of the Series in Yankee Stadium proved to be a struggle. Despite a strong effort by the Dodgers, they lost to the Yankees in Game 1 with a score of 6–5. In Game 2, the Yankees continued their winning streak with a 4–2 win over the Dodgers, who had only two runs for the entire game. At the start of Game 3, the Dodgers increased their determination with a little help from new pitcher Johnny Podres. Putting Podres in proved to be a good move. He held the Yankees to three runs. The Dodgers beat the Yankees in Game 3 with a score of 8–3.

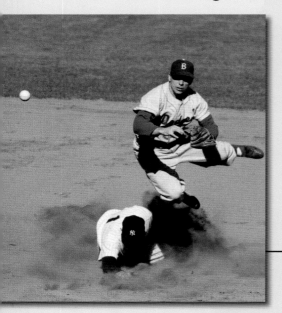

The Dodgers kept their **momentum** going, winning Games 4 and 5. But the cat and mouse game was not over, as the Yankees beat the Dodgers in Game 6 with a score of 5–1. In Game 7, the Dodgers came back with their Game 3 hero, Johnny Podres. Backed by his incredible team, Podres led the Dodgers to a Game 7 win. The team won in Yankee Stadium and captured the World Series title that they had worked so long for!

Shortstop Pee Wee Reese fires the ball to first base.

HISTORY BOX

Baseball in New York

In the 1950s, people who lived outside of New York City had little chance to see a World Series game. During this decade, the New York Yankees played five times against either the Brooklyn Dodgers or the New York Giants. However, with the end of the 1950s came a big change, one that would affect the New York baseball franchises. After the 1957 season, the Dodgers and the Giants moved to California. In 1958, both teams changed their names. The former New York teams were now the Los Angeles Dodgers and the San Francisco Giants.

Jackie Robinson (1919—1972)

In 1947, a University of California—Los Angeles (UCLA) alumni joined the Brooklyn Dodgers. His name was Jackie Robinson, and he was the first African American to play in major league baseball. Robinson's baseball talent and character helped pave the way for progress in the **civil rights** movement. Robinson was an inspiration to fans and to other African Americans.

Robinson was inducted into the Hall of Fame in 1962.

1955 RECORD

Won	Lost	World Series
98	55	Beat New York Yankees 4–3

Hall of Fame

Career Statistics	G	R	H	HR	RBI	SB	BA	Years
Roy Campanella	1,215	627	1,161	242	856	25	.276	1948–1957
Jackie Robinson	1,382	947	1,518	137	734	197	.311	1947–1956
Pee Wee Reese	2,166	1,338	2,170	126	885	232	.269	1940–1958
Duke Snider	2,143	1,259	2,116	407	1,333	99	.295	1947–1964

Pitching Statistics	G	W	L	ERA	SH	Years
Sandy Koufax	397	165	87	2.76	40	1955–1966

Manager: Walter Alston   Won 2,040   Lost 1,613   1954–1976

1961 New York Yankees

In the 1950s the Yankees won the World Series six times. When the 1960s arrived, fans wondered if the Yankees would continue their domination. It certainly looked that way. Even with a rookie manager, Ralph Houk, the Yankees were a strong team. Yogi Berra was still in the outfield. Mickey Mantle was still slugging away on the team, and new talent was also emerging. Roger Maris was one of these new players who had slugger written all over him. He joined the Yankees after the 1959 season.

Members of the 1961 Yankees team pose for a photo.

1961 New York Yankees

C	Elston Howard	LF	Yogi Berra	P	Ralph Terry
1B	Bill Skowron	CF	Mickey Mantle	P	Rollie Sheldon
2B	Bobby Richardson	RF	Roger Maris	P	Jim Coates
3B	Clete Boyer	P	Whitey Ford	P	Buddy Daley
SS	Tony Kubek	P	Bill Stafford	P	Luis Arroyo

Manager: Ralph Houk

Roger Maris was an unusual member of the team. Instead of starting out as a rookie for the New York Yankees, Maris had been **traded** from the Kansas City Athletics team. Having showed that he was a power hitter for the Athletics, Maris continued this strong playing for the Yankees. In his first season, he racked up 39 home runs and 112 RBIs, to finish closely behind Mickey Mantle's 40 home runs. Nicknamed "The M & M boys," Mantle and Maris got fans thinking that they would beat Babe Ruth's record of 60 for single-season home runs.

When Mantle became injured toward the end of the season, Maris was sure he could break Ruth's record. With fans watching every swing of his bat, Maris tied Ruth's record on September 26, 1961. Maris went on to hit home run number 61 in a game against the Boston Red Sox. At the end of the 1961 season, Maris tied Mickey Mantle to lead the American League with 132 runs. He also led the AL with 141 RBIs.

Mickey Mantle (1931–1995)

Mickey Mantle began his major league career when he was only nineteen years old. While playing baseball during high school, Mantle caught the eye of a Yankees' scout. Both his quickness and talent led to him signing a $400 contract with the Yankees. Mantle had such incredible speed that he could run the bases in thirteen seconds. Although Mantle's career was plagued by injuries, he was still an exceptional baseball player. Many wonder what he would have played like if he had been perfectly healthy.

Mantle swings the bat against the Detroit Tigers.

1961 New York Yankees

While their individual players were breaking records, the Yankees team was making history in 1961 as well. They won 109 games in the regular season to establish themselves number one in the American League. Pitcher Whitey Ford had a 25–4 record under his belt, and this 1961 season led him to win the **Cy Young Award** as best pitcher in the AL. With Ford playing his best, the Yankees were more than confident going into the World Series against the Cincinnati Reds.

Yankees' teammates celebrate after winning the 1961 World Series.

In Game 1 of the series at Yankee Stadium, Ford allowed just 2 hits and no runs to lead the Yankees to a 2–0 victory over the Reds. However, Game 2 of the Series wasn't so easy. The Red's ace pitcher Joey Jay held the Yankees. The game ended in a win for the Reds with a score of 6–2. But the Yankees were back to their best in Games 3, 4, and 5. Although they were no longer in their home field, they took the series 4–1 over the Reds. The Yankees had 27 runs in the Series to top the Reds' 13 runs. This was their nineteenth World Series championship!

HISTORY BOX

Baseball on the Move

When the St. Louis Browns became the Baltimore Orioles in 1954 and the Braves moved from Boston to Milwaukee, this signaled a major change in baseball. These were the first two teams in baseball's history to change cities, but they would not be the last. From the late 1950s through the 1970s, a bunch of other teams moved, and still more teams were created. Soon, major league baseball was in Atlanta, Houston, Kansas City, Los Angeles, Oakland, San Diego, Seattle, and many other cities in the United States. Teams even expanded into Canada.

The Yankees went on to capture their twentieth World Series championship in 1962, but lost the next two Series. The Yankees entered the mid-1960s with a team suffering from injuries and with more older players. Mickey Mantle, Roger Maris, Whitey Ford, and other great players tried to play through both injury and older age, but they started to fail. Maris was traded in 1966 to the St. Louis Cardinals, Whitey Ford retired in 1967, and Mickey Mantle retired in 1968. The great age of the Yankees had come to an end. It would be twelve years before the Yankees would get to another championship game. But baseball history had more stars come out of this 1961 Yankees team. Many would go on to be in the Baseball Hall of Fame.

1961 RECORD

Won	Lost	World Series
109	53	Beat Cincinnati Reds 4–1

Hall of Fame

Career Statistics	G	R	H	HR	RBI	SB	BA	Years
Mickey Mantle	2,401	1,677	2,415	536	1,509	153	.298	1951–1968
Yogi Berra	2,120	1,175	2,150	358	1,430	30	.285	1946–1965

Pitching Statistics	G	W	L	ERA	SH	Years
Whitey Ford	498	236	106	2.75	45	1950–1967

When Charlie Finley bought the Kansas City Athletics franchise in 1960, he tried everything to increase fans' interest in the team. He even had the uniforms changed to bright, shiny green and gold colors. The new uniforms did not help the team win games, and Finley eventually moved the team to Oakland, California, before the 1968 season. By 1974, the A's became a part of history. After their move to the west, Finley's team became winners. Some of the A's players would go on to be the best in the decade. Jim "Catfish" Hunter was a star pitcher, and outfielder Reggie Jackson was a young slugger.

This is a photo of Charlie Finley in 1987.

HISTORY BOX

The "Designated Hitter"

In the mid-1960s, Oakland Athletics owner Charlie Finley began talking about changing the rules of baseball so that pitchers would not have to bat. Pitchers sometimes tend to be awful hitters. Finley wanted to make the game more exciting. He thought that by allowing talented hitters to take the pitchers' at bats, this would solve both problems. In 1973, the idea became reality, as the American League adopted the "designated hitter" for the first time. This rule still remains in place today.

1974 Oakland Athletics

C	Ray Fosse	CF	Billy North	P	Dave Hamilton
1B	Gene Tenace	RF	Reggie Jackson	P	Glenn Abbott
2B	Dick Green	DH	Jesus Alou	P	Paul Lindblad
3B	Sal Bando	P	Catfish Hunter	RP	Rollie Fingers
SS	Bert Campaneris	P	Vida Blue		
LF	Joe Rudi	P	Ken Holtzman		

Manager: Alvin Dark

RP=Relief Pitcher

The 1972 Athletics beat the Cincinnati Reds in the World Series to win the championship for the first time since 1930. In 1973, the A's beat the New York Mets to repeat as world champions. While the A's were winning games, they were also making headlines. Stories of fights in the locker room and disagreements with owner Charlie Finley made the entire team **infamous**. The players and Finley seemed to disagree about everything, except for winning games!

Members of the 1974 Athletics team pose for a photo.

The "Angry A's," as they were soon nicknamed, held true to this name. Manager Dick Williams was so fed up with Charlie Finley interfering with how he ran the team that he quit right after the 1973 World Series. It was one of the only times a baseball manager has resigned after winning a championship. Alvin Dark took over the team as manager in 1974 and was determined to lead them to another World Series championship.

1974 Oakland Athletics

Catfish Hunter had a great season, maybe one of the best, as a pitcher. Hunter was even given the Cy Young Award for the 1974 season. He had 25 wins, a 2.49 ERA, and 6 shutouts. In the **bullpen**, the A's relied on closer Rollie Fingers. In baseball today, every team has a bullpen closer—a pitcher who is used only in the eighth or ninth inning of very close games to seal a victory. Back in the early 1970s, this idea of a game-closing pitcher was fairly new. Rollie Fingers was one of the first pitchers who made a Hall of Fame career out of this role.

1974 RECORD

Won	Lost	World Series	AL Championship Series
90	72	Beat Los Angeles Dodgers 4–1	Beat Baltimore Orioles 3–1

Hall of Fame

Career Statistics	G	R	H	HR	RBI	SB	BA	Years
Reggie Jackson	2,820	1,551	2,584	563	1,702	228	.262	1967–1987

Pitching Statistics	G	W	L	ERA	SH	Years
Catfish Hunter	500	224	166	3.26	42	1965–1979
Rollie Fingers	944	114	118	2.90	2	1968–1985

The A's also had third baseman Sal Bando, first baseman Gene Tenace, and outfielder Joe Rudi who were all excellent hitters. In 1974, they returned to the World Series to face the Los Angeles Dodgers in the first ever match-up of two teams from California. The A's won in five games to become the first team other than the Yankees to win three straight World Series championships.

The success of the Athletics soon ended, though. Contract arguments with Charlie Finley led to the team's breakup. Catfish Hunter was the first to go, leaving as a **free agent** to join the New York Yankees on December 31, 1974.

In 1976, Reggie Jackson was gone, and Rollie Fingers followed later that year. But the greatness of the 1974 Oakland Athletics will live on in baseball history, despite the team's "angry" reputation.

Jackson hits a game-winning home run against the Texas Rangers.

Reggie Jackson (1946—   )

Reggie Jackson had not even reached the prime of his career when he won three straight World Series with the 1970s Oakland Athletics. As the Athletics team fell apart, Jackson first went to the Baltimore Orioles, and then to the Yankees. Jackson earned the nickname "Mr. October" for his repeated World Series heroics with both the A's and the Yankees. In Game 6 of the 1977 World Series, Jackson hit 3 home runs in 3 straight at bats, an achievement matched only by Babe Ruth. When he retired in 1987, Jackson ranked number 7 on baseball's all-time home run list, with 563.

1976 Cincinnati Reds

The Red Stockings were created in 1869, giving them the title of baseball's oldest team. But their age hasn't given them championship success, at least not often for the first 75 years of the 20th century. The Reds won a World Series in 1919 that many claim was lost purposely by the opposing Chicago White Sox in a gambling scandal. In 1940, the Reds won the World Series, but lost in 1939 and 1961 to the tough New York Yankees. By the time the 1970s came, the Reds were eager to be Series champions again. With the help of some amazing talent, the Reds became "The Big Red Machine."

In the early 1970s, the Reds had some great hitters in the middle of the batting order. Pete Rose was one of these great hitters. He would eventually be known as baseball's all-time hit king. In 1976, with Pete Rose at third base, Tony Perez at first base, and catcher Johnny Bench, the Reds had all-star hitters at nearly every position. Even outfielders Ken Griffey and George Foster were great hitters.

Members of the 1976 Reds team pose for a photo.

1976 RECORD

Won	Lost	World Series	NL Championship Series
102	60	Beat New York Yankees 4–0	Beat Philadelphia Phillies 3–0

Hall of Fame

Career Statistics	G	R	H	HR	RBI	SB	BA	Years
Johnny Bench	2,158	1,091	2,048	389	1,376	68	.267	1967–1983
Tony Perez	2,777	1,272	2,732	379	1,652	49	.279	1964–1986
Joe Morgan	2,650	1,651	2,518	268	1,134	689	.271	1963–1984

Manager: Sparky Anderson   Won 2,194   Lost 1,834   1970–1995

1976 Cincinnati Reds

C	Johnny Bench	CF	Cesar Geronimo	P	Santo Alcala
1B	Tony Perez	RF	Ken Griffey	P	Don Gullett
2B	Joe Morgan	P	Gary Nolan	P	Pedro Borbon
3B	Pete Rose	P	Pat Zachry	P	Rawley Eastwick
SS	Dave Concepcion	P	Fred Norman		
LF	George Foster	P	Jack Billingham		

Manager: Sparky Anderson

In 1976, the Big Red Machine had 8 regular players that would make 64 All-Star appearances, win 26 **Gold Glove** awards, and 6 league MVP awards. Many baseball fans still consider the starting eight players of the 1976 Reds to be among the greatest of all time. The Reds led the National League in every team-batting category, scoring almost 100 more runs than any other team. The Reds went 102–60 in the 1976 regular season, with George Foster leading the NL in RBIs with 121, and Rose leading in hits with 215.

1976 Cincinnati Reds

During the League Championship Series (a second layer of playoffs that was added in 1969) the Reds beat the Philadelphia Phillies, who went 101–61 during their regular season. The Reds swept the Series, beating the Phillies in three games. When the Big Red Machine went on to the World Series, the New York Yankees were waiting for them.

Johnny Bench waits for a runner during the 1976 World Series.

HISTORY BOX

Baseball Hall of Fame

The **Baseball Hall of Fame** was originally founded in 1936. The first five players inducted into the Hall of Fame were Babe Ruth, Ty Cobb, Honus Wagner, Christy Mathewson, and Walter Johnson. The actual National Baseball Hall of Fame and Museum opened in 1939, in Cooperstown, New York. The museum has a collection of items from baseball history. In order to be voted into the Hall of Fame, a player must be retired from baseball for at least five years. Future members of the Hall of Fame are voted on by the Baseball Writers Association of America; an organization that also chooses the winner of the Cy Young Award.

It was a tough match-up, but with a home field advantage the Reds beat the Yankees in Game 1. However, the Yankees fought back in Game 2 and the Reds had a close call with a loss of 4–3. Back in New York, the Reds went on to win Games 3 and 4 by a combined score of 13–4. The Yankees, who only led four innings of the entire Series, were beaten. The Big Red Machine, with powerful Johnny Bench, grabbed the World Series championship. They became the first National League team to win back-to-back World Series since the 1921–1922 New York Giants.

Rose hits a pop fly ball against the NY Mets.

Pete Rose (1941–   )

Nicknamed "Charlie Hustle," Pete Rose was baseball's greatest contact hitter. He had a .303 career batting average and a major league record of 4,256 hits in his 24-year career that began in 1963. However, controversy ended Rose's career in 1989 when he was manager of the Reds. Rose was banned from the game for gambling on baseball. For years, Rose denied gambling, but in 2004 he finally admitted to it. He has yet to be let back into baseball, even though he has asked to come back several times.

1998 New York Yankees

After winning two World Series in 1977 and 1978, the New York Yankees entered a fifteen-year stretch without a championship trophy. It was the longest stretch in Yankees history. When Joe Torre took over as manager of the Yankees in 1996, he immediately brought a sense of trust and discipline to the team. With Torre's help, the Yankees were ready to be on top of baseball again.

After a win in the 1996 World Series, the Yankees lost in the opening round of the 1997 playoffs to the Cleveland Indians. Major league baseball in 1998 was filled with a lot of exciting events. The Chicago Cubs' Sammy Sosa and the St. Louis Cardinals' Mark McGwire were chasing and breaking Roger Maris' single-season home run record. To top it off, the mighty New York Yankees were back and better than ever. That year they did what everyone thought was impossible. They topped the 1927 "Murderers' Row" team.

1998 RECORD

Won	Lost	World Series
114	48	Beat San Diego Padres 4–0

AL Championship Series
Beat Cleveland Indians 4–2

AL Division Series
Beat Texas Rangers 3–0

1998 Team Statistics

Player (position)	G	R	H	HR	RBI	SB	BA	Age
Jorge Posada (C)	111	56	96	17	63	0	.268	26
Tino Martinez (1B)	142	92	149	28	123	2	.281	30
Chuck Knoblauch (2B)	150	117	160	17	64	31	.265	29
Scott Brosius (3B)	152	86	159	19	98	11	.300	31
Derek Jeter (SS)	149	127	203	19	84	30	.324	24
Chad Curtis (LF)	151	79	111	10	56	21	.243	29
Bernie Williams (CF)	128	101	169	26	97	15	.339	29
Paul O'Neill (RF)	152	95	191	24	116	15	.317	35
Darryl Strawberry (DH)	101	44	73	24	57	8	.247	36

Shortstop Derek Jeter led the American League in runs scored, and center fielder Bernie Williams led the AL in batting. Jeter and Williams joined first baseman Tito Williams and right fielder Paul O'Neill to provide the foundation for the highest-scoring team in baseball. Jeter rose to the top as the captain of the team. While most shortstops are expected to concentrate mostly on fielding, Jeter was an excellent fielder and a **clutch hitter**. In 1998, his third year in the major leagues, he had a .324 average.

Jeter hits a home run against the Seattle Mariners.

Derek Jeter (1974–   )

Born in New Jersey, Derek Jeter is one of the most talented players in baseball. He began his career as a shortstop with the New York Yankees in 1995. Jeter was so impressive in his first year that he earned the rookie of the year title for major league baseball. His impressive character both on and off the field led to him being named Yankees' captain on June 3, 2003.

The 1998 Yankees team started off their season great. On May 17, pitcher David Wells pitched a perfect game against the Minnesota Twins. Wells, who once wore Babe Ruth's baseball cap in a game, got out all 27 batters he faced. With Wells, and more confidence than ever, the Yankees finished their season with a record 114 wins. This was 22 wins ahead of second-place Boston Red Sox. Even the 1927 Yankees with their "Murderers' Row" didn't do this. The Yankees went on to win 11 more times in the post-season, bringing their total to 125 wins. This record has never been matched.

Scott Brosius hits against the Cleveland Indians in Game 2 of the AL Championship Series.

HISTORY BOX

The Great Duel

After the strike that canceled the 1994 World Series, major league baseball lost hundreds of thousands of fans. Football became more popular than baseball. Baseball fans were tired of players fighting with owners over huge salaries. Baseball needed something big to get its fans back. That big thing came in 1998. Two sluggers, Mark McGwire, with the St. Louis Cardinals, and Sammy Sosa, with the Chicago Cubs, dueled for the single-season home run record that summer. McGwire reached 61 first, and finished with 70 home runs. Sosa hit 66 home runs for the season.

The 1998 New York Yankees celebrate their 112th victory, which sets a new American League record.

1998 New York Yankees

C	Jorge Posada	CF	Bernie Williams	P	Hideki Irabu
1B	Tino Martinez	RF	Paul O'Neill	P	Orlando Hernandez
2B	Chuck Knoblauch	DH	Darryl Strawberry	P	Mariano Rivera
3B	Scott Brosius	P	Andy Pettitte	P	Mike Stanton
SS	Derek Jeter	P	David Wells	P	Graeme Lloyd
LF	Chad Curtis	P	David Cone	P	Darren Holmes

Manager: Joe Torre

In the opening round of the playoffs, the Yankees swept the Texas Rangers and then beat the Cleveland Indians in a tough six games to win the League Championship Series. The World Series against the San Diego Padres proved to be easy. After Tino Martinez hit a grand slam in the first game, the Yankees beat the Padres 9–6.

Yankees' third baseman Scott Brosius had 2 home runs in Game 3 and went on to be named the Series' Most Valuable Player. Ace reliever Mariano Rivera saved three of the four games without allowing a run and the Yankees took the Padres in four games. The Yankees went on to win the next 2 World Series titles, including a record 26th in 2000 over the New York Mets. The 1998 New York Yankees team is thought to be the best team of the modern game.

Did you know that the Boston Red Sox won the first ever World Series in 1903? They beat the Pittsburgh Pirates 4–3 and became the first World Series champions. The team was a force in the early 1900s, winning a number of Series up through 1918. But then they did something that will go down in history. They traded a pitcher named Babe Ruth to the New York Yankees in 1920. With Ruth's help, the Yankees became an unstoppable baseball team and made their mark in history. But without Ruth, the Boston Red Sox team stopped winning World Series championships. Many fans believed that selling Ruth had brought a curse to the team.

ARROYO

BELLHORN

CABRERA

DAMON

EMBREE

FOULKE

The 2004 Red Sox fought hard to break the curse.

FRANCONA

KAPLER

LOWE

LESKANIC

MARTINEZ

MIENTKIEWICZ

2004 Boston Red Sox

C	Jason Varitek	LF	Manny Ramirez	P	Bronson Arroyo
1B	Kevin Millar	CF	Johnny Damon	P	Derek Lowe
2B	Mark Bellhorn	RF	Gabe Kapler	P	Pedro Martinez
3B	Bill Mueller	DH	David Ortiz	P	Tim Wakefield
SS	Pokey Reese	P	Curt Schilling		

Manager: Terry Francona

The 2004 Boston Red Sox were determined to break the curse and win another World Series championship. However, they would need to defeat the New York Yankees in the AL Championship Series first. The Red Sox had some great talent to do this. The outfield was made up of strong players such as left fielder Manny Ramirez, right fielder Gabe Kapler, and center fielder Johnny Damon. Ramirez had a .308 BA and Damon had a .304 BA for the 2004 season. Designated hitter David Ortiz was strong as well, with a .301 BA. The Red Sox definitely had the hitting and fielding talent to make it to the championship.

HISTORY BOX

The Curse

In the six years that Babe Ruth played for Boston, the Red Sox won three World Series championships. When Ruth was sold to the Yankees for $125,000 and a $300,000 loan to the owner of the Red Sox, the team stopped winning World Series. In fact, 1918 was the last Series that the Sox won. Many thought that getting rid of Babe Ruth had laid a curse on the Boston Red Sox. They called it the "Curse of the Bambino", after Ruth's nickname. When Boston won in 2004, many thought the curse had finally been lifted. What do you think?

During the 2004 regular season, the Red Sox and the Yankees battled it out in the American League, with the Yankees having a record 101–61 over the Red Sox 98–64. In the post-season, it was a different story. After earning a **wild-card** entry into the division playoffs, the Red Sox swept the Anaheim Angels in three games. They were excited about their win, but nervous as well. They would have to face the Yankees in the League Championship Series.

2004 Boston Red Sox

The League Championship Series started out badly for the Red Sox. The Yankees beat them in the first three games, winning Game 3 by the embarrassing score of 19–8. In Game 4, Boston was close to defeat. They were in the ninth inning with the Yankees beating them 4–3. Three outs from elimination the Red Sox were able to tie the game. Finally, in the twelfth inning, the Red Sox beat the Yankees with a homer by David Ortiz.

The Red Sox continued chasing the championship. In the fifth game, Ortiz hit a two-run homer in the eighth inning to tie the game, and in the fourteenth inning the Red Sox again beat the Yankees. In Game 6, ace pitcher Curt Schilling gave Boston a win. Game 7 was the icing on the cake, with the Red Sox beating the Yankees for the American League championship.

Mark Bellhorn hits a home run in Game 1 of the World Series.

The Red Sox were on a roll, all the way to the World Series. The St. Louis Cardinals were no match against the Red Sox—confident after beating their enemy the Yankees. Game 1 of the Series ended with the Red Sox defeating the Cardinals 11–9. Game 2 was even more intense. Starting pitcher Curt Schilling played through an ankle injury that left his sock bloody. Again, determination won them another game. Schilling was a hero, allowing the Cardinals only two hits in Game 2. The Red Sox beat the Cardinals 6–2.

Pedro Martinez (1971–)

Traded to the Boston Red Sox in 1997, Pedro Martinez has made his mark with his great pitching. Martinez was born in the Dominican Republic, and started his baseball career at a young age. When he was just fifteen years old, Martinez pitched for the Dominican Republic national team in the Summer Olympics. With Martinez' great pitching, the Boston Red Sox were able to win their first World Series championship since 1918.

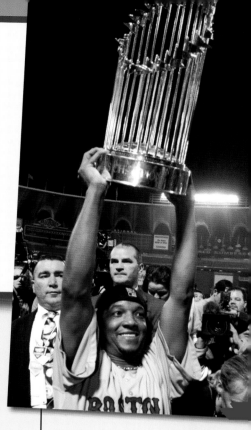

Pedro Martinez holds up the championship trophy after Boston wins the World Series.

Game 3 proved easy for the Red Sox, too. They beat the Cardinals 4–1 and went on to Game 4 closer to a title. In this final game, the Red Sox sealed their fate. They beat the St. Louis Cardinals 3–0. With eight consecutive post-season wins over the Yankees and Cardinals, the 2004 Boston Red Sox were finally World Series champions. After 86 years without a championship, the curse was finally broken!

2004 RECORD

Won	Lost	World Series
98	64	Beat St. Louis Cardinals 4–0

AL Championship Series
Beat New York Yankees 4–3

AL Division Series
Beat Anaheim Angels 3–0

2004 Team Statistics

Player (position)	G	R	H	HR	RBI	SB	BA	Age
Jason Varitek (C)	137	67	137	18	73	10	.296	32
Kevin Millar (1B)	150	74	151	18	74	1	.297	32
Mark Bellhorn (2B)	138	93	138	17	82	6	.264	29
Bill Mueller (3B)	110	75	113	12	57	2	.283	33
Pokey Reese (SS)	96	32	54	3	29	6	.221	31
Manny Ramirez (LF)	152	108	175	43	130	2	.308	32
Johnny Damon (CF)	150	123	189	20	94	19	.304	30
Gabe Kapler (RF)	136	51	79	6	33	5	.272	28
David Ortiz (DH)	150	94	175	41	139	0	.301	28

The Final Score

So what makes a great baseball team? You have read about record-breaking players, unbeatable starting lineups, and dedicated managers. From the 1907 Chicago Cubs to the 2004 Boston Red Sox, the talent that goes into a history-making team is unbelievable at times. After decades have gone by, players such as Babe Ruth, Mickey Mantle, Whitey Ford, and Pete Rose still have a huge place in baseball history. Newer players such as Derek Jeter and Pedro Martinez continue to rise in the ranks and will earn a place in the record books as well.

Every year, baseball produces talent and sets new records. Games are played that surprise fans and keep them coming back for more. The 2004 World Series champions, the Boston Red Sox, proved that a "curse" could be broken when they defeated the New York Yankees in the American League playoffs. Players such as Barry Bonds, Sammy Sosa, and Mark McGwire all broke Roger Maris' record for most home runs in a season. As baseball moves forward the level of the game advances, too.

Baseball is truly a team sport. Teams can have outstanding players, but what makes them successful is their ability to come together and play great baseball. Managers inspire players, who turn around and inspire fans. Baseball continues to be a fantastic sport, both for children who play in little leagues through to the major league players of today. Baseball continues to produce great teams who earn their place in history.

Barry Bonds waves to fans after hitting a home run.

Timeline

1869: The Cincinnati Red Stockings become the first professional baseball team.

1903: The World Series is created to determine the best major league baseball team each year.

1907: Chicago Cubs win the World Series against the Detroit Tigers 4–1–0.

1927: Babe Ruth hits a record 60 home runs and the New York Yankees win the World Series against the Pittsburgh Pirates 4–0.

1935: Major league baseball has its first night game in Cincinnati.

1942: St. Louis Cardinals win the World Series against the New York Yankees 4–1.

1947: Jackie Robinson is the first African American to play in major league baseball.

1953: New York Yankees win the World Series against the Brooklyn Dodgers 4–2.

1955: Brooklyn Dodgers win the World Series against the New York Yankees 4–3.

1961: Roger Maris breaks Ruth's home run record.

1961: New York Yankees win the World Series against the Cincinnati Reds 4–1.

1974: Oakland Athletics win the World Series against the Los Angeles Dodgers 4–1.

1976: Cincinnati Reds win the World Series against the New York Yankees 4–0.

1998: New York Yankees win the World Series against the San Diego Padres 4–0.

2001: San Francisco Giants' player Barry Bonds sets a new record for home runs in a season with 73.

2004: Boston Red Sox win the World Series against the St. Louis Cardinals 4–0.

New York Yankees' fans cheer in the 1998 World Series.

Glossary

ace team's best starting or closing pitcher

American League (AL) one of the two professional leagues in major league baseball

Baseball Hall of Fame organization that honors the best baseball players throughout history. Usually, players are inducted into the Hall of Fame years after they stop playing or have died.

batting average (BA) measure of batting ability calculated as the number of base hits divided by number of at bats

bullpen relief pitchers on a baseball team. It can also refer to the area where the relief pitchers warm up before they play in the game.

civil rights personal freedoms guaranteed to all Americans by the Constitution of the United States

clutch hitter hitter who comes through in tough situations

Cy Young Award award given by the Baseball Writers Association of America to the most outstanding pitcher in each league, in honor of Hall of Famer, Cy Young

dominant leader. A dominant team is one that wins lots of games and seems unbeatable.

double play play in which two outs are made

earned run average (ERA) measure of how many runs a pitcher allows over a nine inning game. The formula is (earned runs times 9) divided by innings pitched.

franchise professional sports team organization. For example, the New York Yankees is a franchise.

free agent player who is legally free to sign a contract with any team

Gold Glove award given to the best fielder in each position in each league. Managers and coaches give this award.

grand slam home run with runners on all three bases that results in four runs scored

infamous being well-known for a bad quality

League Championship Series (LCS) best-of-seven game series used to find the League champion. The winners of each of these series go on to play against each other in the World Series.

major league group of the country's best baseball teams

momentum driving force that keeps you going

National League (NL) one of the two professional leagues in major league baseball

pennant symbol that represents winning the league championship

playoff one of the post-season games used to determine the league champions

precision something that is exact or accurate

rookie player or manager in his first season in the major leagues

runs batted in (RBI) given to a batter when one or more runners score as a result of a base hit or any other hit that drives a run in

shutout game in which one team fails to score a run. It is also the statistic given to a pitcher who starts and finishes a game in which the opposing team does not score a run.

slugger powerful hitting batter who makes many extra base hits and home runs

sweep when a team wins all the games of a series

trade exchange of players between two teams

wild-card team allowed to compete in the Division Championship Series without winning a division title because it has the best win-loss record of any of the remaining teams in the league

Further reading

Campbell, Peter A. *Old Time Baseball and the First Modern World Series.*
Minneapolis: Millbrook Press Incorporated, 2002

Gilbert, Thomas W. *The Soaring Twenties: Babe Ruth and the Home Run Decade.* Danbury, CT: Scholastic Library Publishing, 2000

Helmer, Diana Star, and Thomas S. Owens. *The History of Baseball.*
New York: The Rosen Publishing Group, 2000

Thornley, Stew. *Super Sports Star Barry Bonds.*
Berkeley Heights, NJ: Enslow Publishers Inc., 2004

Wienstein, Howard. *Mickey Mantle.*
New York: The Rosen Publishing Group, 2004

Addresses

National Baseball Hall of Fame and Museum
25 Main Street
Cooperstown, NY 13326
www.baseballhalloffame.org

Legends of the Game Baseball Museum
1000 Ballpark Way Suite 400
Arlington, Texas 76011

Major League Baseball Official Site
www.mlb.com

Index

African-American players 23

American League (AL) 4, 7, 14, 17, 18, 25, 26, 28, 37, 41, 42, 44

Baltimore Orioles 27, 31

Baseball Hall of Fame 5, 34

Baseball Writers Association of America 34

batting average (BA) 8

Beazely, Johnny 15

Berra, Yogi 17, 18, 19, 24, 27

Bonds, Barry 44

Boston Red Sox 5, 10, 25, 38, 40–43, 44

Brooklyn Dodgers 18, 20–23

Brown, Mordecai 6, 8, 9

bullpen closer 30

Chicago Cubs 5, 6–9, 37, 38

Chicago White Sox 7, 32

Cincinnati Reds 26, 29, 32–35

civil rights movement 23

Cleveland Browns 18

Cleveland Indians 37, 39

clutch hitters 37

Cobb, Ty 8, 34

Combs, Earle 10, 11, 13

Cooper, Mort 15

curveball 6

Cy Young Award 26, 30, 34

designated hitters 28, 41

Detroit Tigers 8

DiMaggio, Joe 16

divisions 4

earned run average (ERA) 6

Evers, Johnny 7, 9

Fingers, Rollie 30, 31

Ford, Whitey 17, 18, 19, 26, 27, 44

franchises 6, 8, 10, 19, 22, 28

gambling 32, 35

Gold Glove awards 33

grand slams 18, 39

Griffey, Ken 32

Kansas City Athletics 25

League Championship Series (LCS) 5, 34, 39, 41, 42

Los Angeles Dodgers 22, 30

McGwire, Mark 37, 38, 44

major league baseball 4, 17, 27, 37, 44

managers 5, 9, 18, 19, 29, 44

Mantle, Mickey 16–17, 19, 24, 25, 27, 44

Martinez, Pedro 40, 43, 44

Martinez, Tino 39

MVP awards 33

National League (NL) 4, 6, 7, 14–15, 18, 20, 21, 33

New York Giants 22, 35

New York Mets 29, 39

New York Yankees 10–13, 15, 16–19, 20, 22, 24–27, 30, 35, 36–39, 40, 41, 42, 44

Oakland Athletics 28–31

pennants 6

Philadelphia Phillies 34

Pittsburgh Pirates 13, 40

playoffs 4, 34, 37, 39, 41, 44

Podres, Johnny 22

Ruth, "Babe" (George Herman) 10–11, 13, 16, 25, 31, 34, 38, 40, 41, 44

St. Louis Browns 27

St. Louis Cardinals 13, 14–15, 27, 37, 38, 42, 43

San Diego Padres 39

San Francisco Giants 5, 22

shutouts 8, 15

Slaughter, Enos 14

sluggers 16, 24, 28, 38

Stengel, Casey 18, 19

televised games 17

Tenace, Gene 30

Texas Rangers 39

Tinker, Joe 7, 9

Torre, Joe 36

wild-card entries 41

Williams, Tito 37